JJ

Parker, Nancy Win-
slow

Love from Aunt
Betty

DATE DUE

| | | | |
|---|---|---|---|
| | | | |
| | | | |
| | | | |
| | | | |
| | | | |
| | | | |
| | | | |
| | | | |
| | | | |
| | | | |
| | | | |

# LOVE FROM AUNT BETTY

# LOVE FROM AUNT BETTY

### Nancy Winslow Parker

**Dodd, Mead & Company • New York**

Copyright © 1983 by Nancy Winslow Parker
Printed in the United States of America

1   2   3   4   5   6   7   8   9   10

Library of Congress Cataloging in Publication Data

Parker, Nancy Winslow.
Love from Aunt Betty

Summary: Aunt Betty sends Charlie an old Transylvanian
gypsy recipe for chocolate fudge cake which calls for
cobwebs and dried Carpathian tree toad flakes.
[1. Humorous stories.   2. Cake—Fiction]   I. Title.
PZ7.P2274Lm  1983       [E]       82-45988
ISBN 0-396-08135-5

*To Seascape's Dylan*

Dear Charlie,

I know how much you like to cook,

so I am sending you this recipe
for Chocolate Fudge Cake.

I found it in an old trunk in the basement wrapped around this dusty green bottle marked "Dried Carpathian Tree Toads."

Uncle Clyde brought it back from Transylvania many years ago. It was given to him by an aged Gypsy woman who lived in the mountains.

The directions are simple.
Heat chocolate, eggs, and milk.

Then blend sugar, shortening, and vanilla.

Sift flour, baking soda, and salt. To this
add one large cobweb.

Most of the ingredients can be found in your mother's kitchen pantry.

Mix everything together with a few
flakes of the dried tree toads.

Bake in oven at 350°
for 30 minutes.

You might want to try a butter cream icing...

...if the cake is too dry.

Lots of luck!

Love from Aunt Betty

DOG